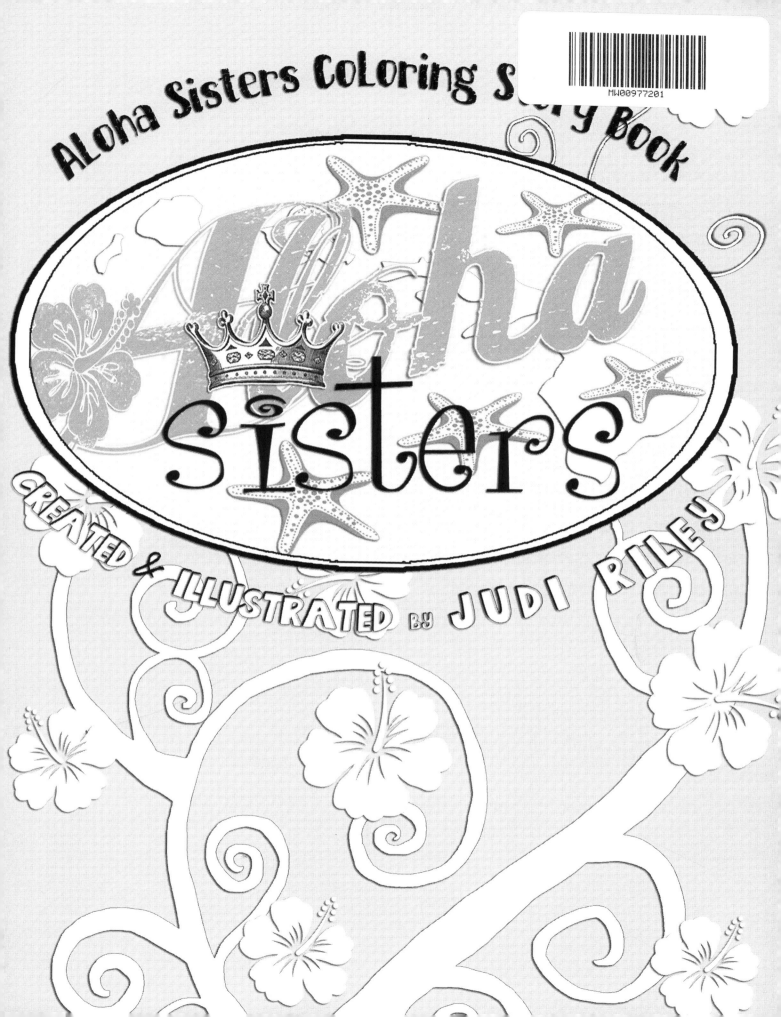

Aloha Sisters Coloring Story Book

Aloha Sisters

CREATED & ILLUSTRATED BY JUDI RILEY

Look for more Tiki Tales books:

The Original Merkins: A Field Journal
The Original Aerkins: A Field Journal
How to Live Aloha, starring Oink & Moo
How to Live Mermaid, starring Oink & Moo
How to Live Surfer, starring Oink & Moo
When I am Quiet on Maui
When I am Quiet on Oʻahu
When I am Quiet on Kauaʻi
When I am Quiet on Big Island
When I am Quiet on Lānaʻi
Absolutely Awesome Island Animals

Find the Aloha Sisters doll collection
at AlohaSisters.com

Visit www.TikiTales.com

First Edition

ISBN-13: 978-1975651671
ISBN-10: 1975651677
Printed and bound in USA

Dedicated to the original Aloha Sisters

Margit, Shay, Robin, Cris & Leolani,

who taught me to dream up a fairy tale, and then swim into it.

KAIMANA

KUKUI

KANANI

LEHUA

LEOLANI

Leolani

Kukui

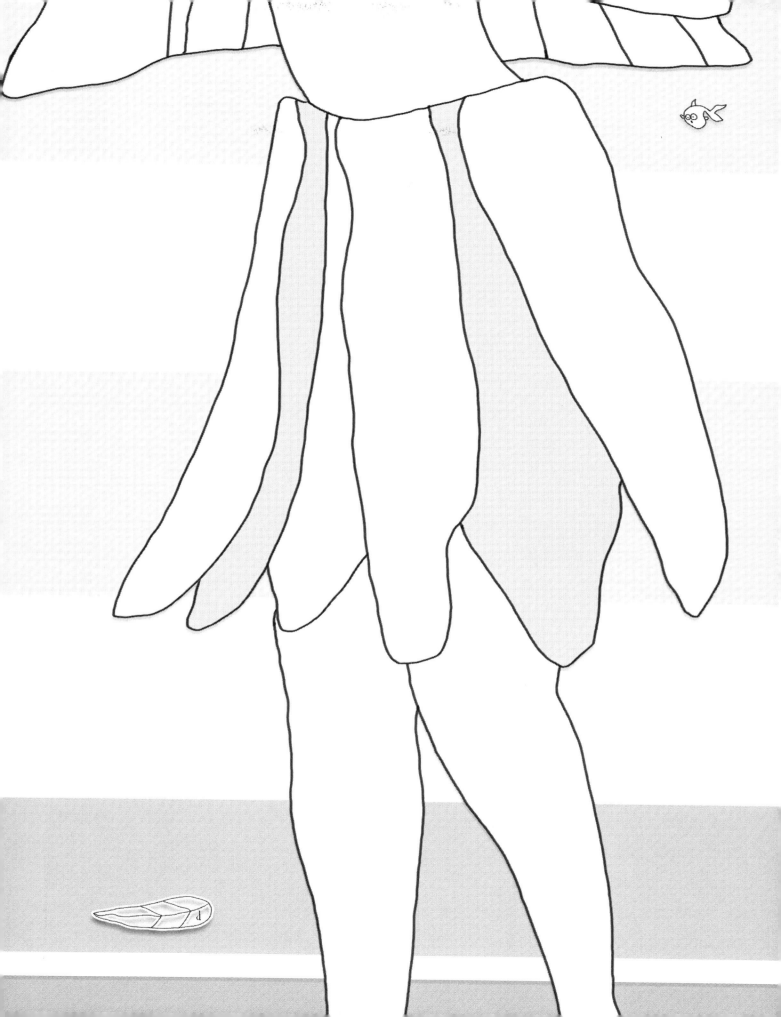

LEHUA

KANANI

KAIMANA

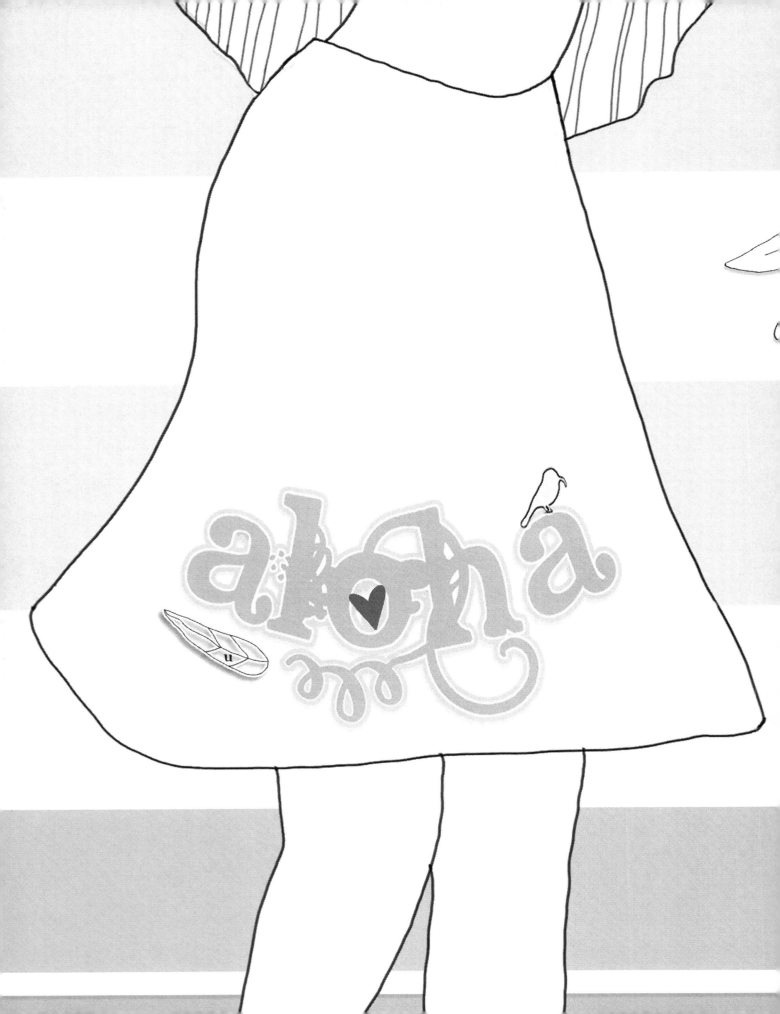

LEOLANI

MerLar Bear

MerLaLa

MerRangutan

Merlggy

MerCess

MerAerEe

Merpotamus

MerUnny

AerLephant

AerOth

AerGer

AerFish

AerFish

AerFish

Aerlno

AerBrush

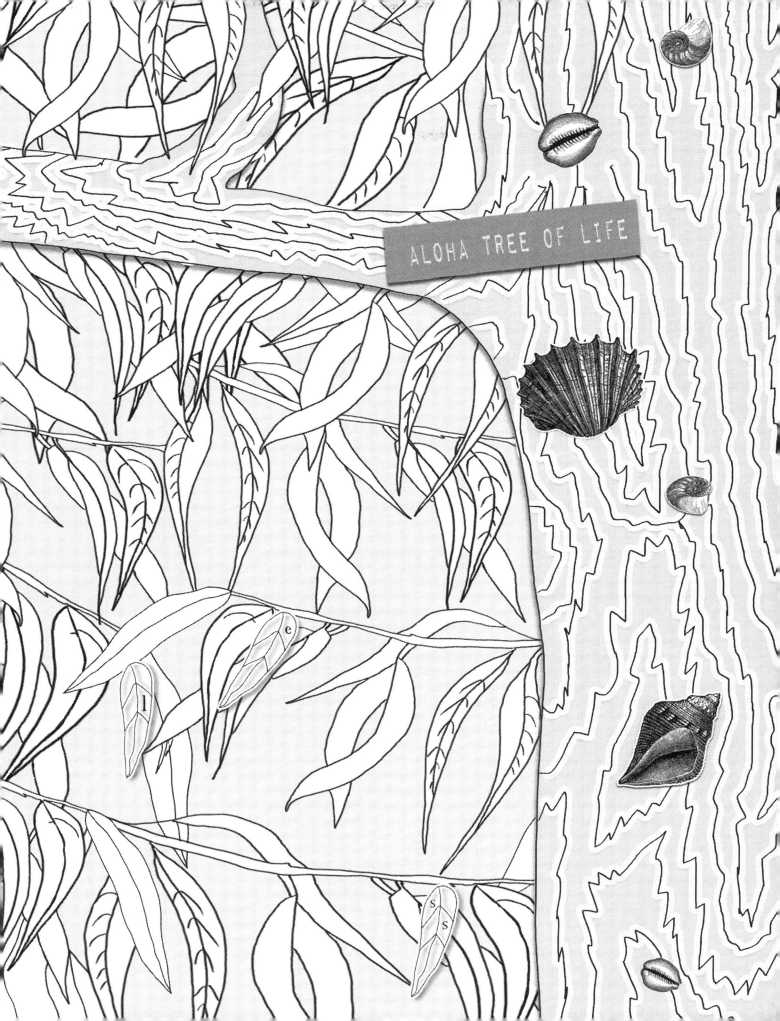

ALOHA TREE OF LIFE

My ♡ Dreams

Sisters help my dreams take flight

Do something today to give my Sisters feathers for their dreams.

GS: Aloha Sister Thank you for being the very best sister you could be from the day I was born. Thank you for always inspiring me to become my best self. Thank you for Loving me so perfectly. I love you forever. Aloha, your sister KC

HB: Aloha Sister, I blew out the candles on my birthday cake
and wished for a baby Sister who would be my Forever Friend.
Sisters Forever. Aloha Sister, JB
p. s. I am still the Queen.

Aloha

My Letter to my Sister
Aloha Sister,

Aloha, xo Sister

alohasisters.com · made on Maui & Lana'i by children's author Judi Riley

KAIMANA · LEHUA · KANANI · KUKUI · LEOLANI

Made on Maui & Lana'i

our eco friendly fabric is made in the USA

Alohasisters

alohasisters.com

Love ♥

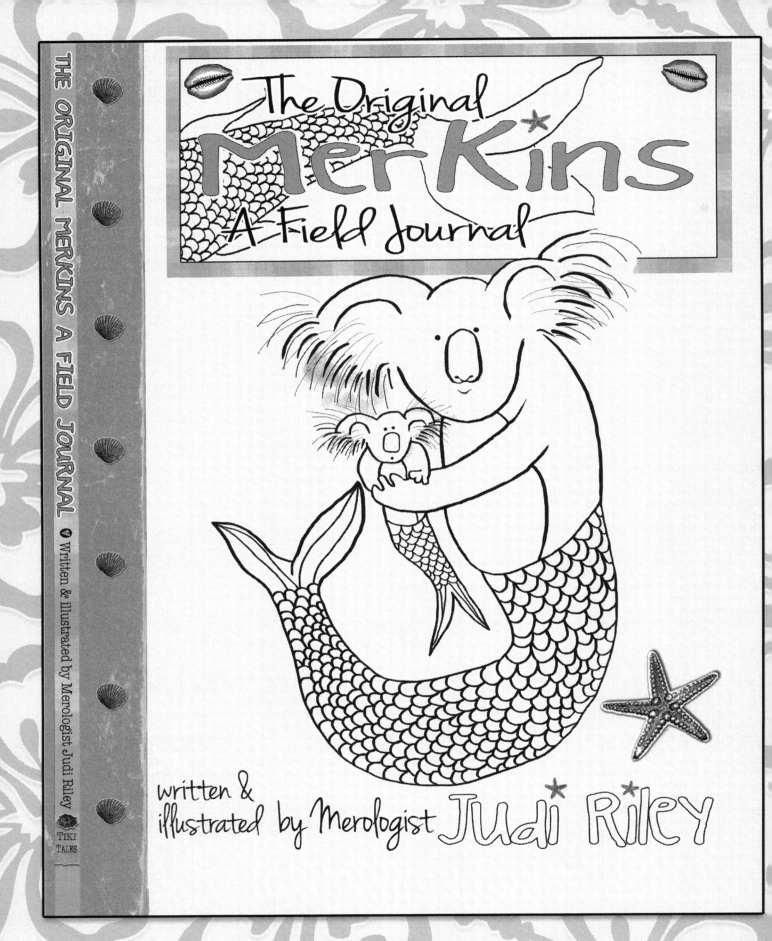

The Original MerKins
A Field Journal

written &
illustrated by Merologist Judi Riley

A New Release by Judi Riley, "The Original MerKins: A Field Journal"

Made in the USA
Columbia, SC
03 July 2022

62743757R00026